Heirloom Trilogy

PRINCESS *Terra* AND KING ABADDON

PRINCESS *Vinnea* AND THE GULAVORES

PRINCESS *Mariana* AND LIXO ISLAND

INAUGURAL SERIES: STORIES 1-3
OF THE
GUARDIAN PRINCESSES

This book was produced by the collective work of the Guardian Princess Alliance.

Written by Setsu Shigematsu and Ashanti McMillon

Editorial Assistance:
Ilse Ackerman
Kelsey Moore
Rié Collett
Ron Collett
Nausheen Sheikh
Pachet Bryant
Realista Rodriguez

Illustrated by A. Das
Preliminary sketches for *Princess Terra*: Leon Chen, Angela Eir,
Yang Liu, Kayla Madison, and Nicole Phung
For *Princess Vinnea*: Mindy Vong
For *Princess Mariana*: Dalia Quiroz and Michelle Le
Wardrobe Design: Kayla Madison, Sophia Wu, and Nausheen Sheikh

Cover and layout by Vikram Sangha
Common Core questions by Tracy Hualde
Reading level assessment by Candice Herron

ISBN: 978-0-9913194-3-5
Library of Congress Control Number: 2014930083

Table of Contents

The Alliance

The Guardian Princess Alliance (GPA) is an organization committed to educating and empowering children to make a difference in the world. Our organization began as an initiative aiming to positively transform the cultural meaning of the princess. The Guardian Princess Alliance is a growing community of parents, educators, students, artists, and professionals who share a common goal of creating better role models for children through our stories.

The Guardian Princess stories represent princesses as inspiring leaders who protect the people and the planet. Our diverse princesses model compassion and intelligence, and demonstrate the power of knowledge and collective action. Our magical stories promote racial, cultural, and gender diversity. Themes include healthy living, greater care for the environment, and peaceful conflict resolution.

We want to foster a healthy self-esteem based on the development of children's talents and helping others. We seek to cultivate ethical principles and knowledge that will inspire readers to create a better world for future generations. Each story includes discussion questions to assess comprehension, a glossary that expands a child's vocabulary, and an etymology chart to enrich knowledge of different languages.

These books were produced through the collective work of the following
Guardian Princess Alliance members:
Setsu Shigematsu, Founder • Ashanti McMillon, Co-Founder • Rié Collett, Executive Director

A. Das • Al Dupont • Amalia Cabezas • Carrie Meng • Eli PaintedCrow • Ilse Ackerman
Jason Lin • Kayla Madison • Kelsey Moore • Lancy Zhang • Nausheen Sheikh
Neill Chua • Nicole Phung • Nilou Moochhala • Pachet Bryant
Raymond Gutierrez • Realista Rodriguez • Sandy Liang • Sophia Wu
Stephanie Cordero • Tracy Hualde • Vianey Ramirez Roseborough • Vikram Sangha

ETYMOLOGY CHART

Etymology: the origin of a word

Name	Language	Meaning
Amel	Arabic	hope, derived from Amal
Armonía	Latin/Spanish	joint, agreement; harmony (pronounced ar·mo·NEE·ah)
Feliz	Latin/Portuguese	happy; derived from the Latin word *felix*
Fulsi	Latin	shines
Iris	Greek/Latin	rainbow
Lixo	Latin/Portuguese	garbage; waste (pronounced LEE·shoo)
Mariana	Hebrew Latin	related to Mary/Maria; associated with *stella maris*, star of the sea
Renova	Latin/Portuguese	renews; restores
Spuma	Latin	foam, slime
Sujo	Portuguese	dirty (pronounced SOO·zhoo)

GLOSSARY

Ancestors: people who are related to you who lived a long time ago

Bountiful: large in quantity; plentiful

Conch shell: the shell of a type of tropical mollusk that is usually brightly colored with a spiral shape; it may be used as a type of wind instrument

Harmony: to be in agreement; to have a peaceful, friendly relationship

Marine life: plants and animals that live in the oceans, lakes, and rivers

Pollution: putting unclean, dirty, or harmful things that don't belong somewhere in an environment (for example, smog is a kind of air pollution)

Ponder: to carefully think about something

Recycle: to make something new from something that has been used before; to process used objects (for example, glass, cans, or paper) into new material

Waste: material left over, rejected, or thrown away

Dedications

Dedicated to those who protect the people and the planet.

Especially...

Alessia Belanga

Nisreen and Akbar Firdosy

Dionna Klein

Emi Klein

Elijah Klein

Sayaka Rodriguez

Taer Rodriguez

Kate Smith Scalero

Sam Smith Scalero

Tiffany So-Lee

Stephanie So-Lee

PRINCESS Terra AND KING ABADDON

WRITTEN BY
SETSU SHIGEMATSU
& THE GUARDIAN PRINCESS ALLIANCE

ILLUSTRATED BY A. DAS

NCE UPON A TIME in a land called Primos, there lived a princess named Terra. She had wavy golden hair and sparkling green eyes. Princess Terra was the Guardian of the Land. It was her role to protect and care for the land that she loved so dearly. She cherished the flowers, the orchards, and the gardens. She would talk and sing to the beautiful plants and trees. Through her songs, she expressed thanks for the food and wonderful fruits of the land. She thanked the plants for making clean air that kept the people of Primos healthy and happy. Princess Terra would sing:

O Nature so beautiful and bright
Your sun warms us all with its shining light
Meadows of green wonder, fields of golden wheat
Thank you for your wholesome food we eat
Trees of Primos that give us shelter and care
Thank you for the fruit you share

Princess Terra lived among farmers who worked very hard every morning in the fields and orchards. They loved to plant seeds and harvest fruits and vegetables from the bountiful land. Their hard work and fresh food made the people healthy and strong.

In the afternoons, the farmers always made time for some good fun. They would sing:

We love to work hard, and we love to have fun

We dance and play under the big, bright sun

We play with our lutes, wooden flutes, and chimes

With each note in harmony and lyrics that rhyme

We hold festivals to celebrate the changing of the seasons

Our love of the land and music gives us reason

One day, as autumn approached and the leaves turned from green to beautiful shades of yellow, orange, and red, Princess Terra was walking through the woods and came across some strange holes in the ground.

The farmers of Primos would never dig into the Earth with such carelessness. Princess Terra thought to herself, *How unusual. I wonder where these holes came from.* She knelt down to scoop a handful of soil and sang:

> *Sediments, minerals, and deposits of clay*
> *Let the land be healed and loved every day*

She poured the soil from her hand and refilled the holes. Happy that the land was restored, Princess Terra smiled and walked back to the village square.

That same day, while some children of Primos were playing in the woods, they saw a strange man. He was wearing a grey suit that had steel spikes on the shoulders. He had a big crooked grin. As he walked through the land of Primos, he was digging holes everywhere with his strange metal machine.

When Princess Terra heard from the children about this man, she went to the woods to find him.

Upon finding him, Princess Terra kindly said, "Welcome to Primos. What brings you here, and why are you digging holes in our land?"

The man said, "I am Chief Officer Dracos. I have been sent by the mighty King Abaddon, whose power extends across many lands. He is the ruler of Voracity, a land of riches, robots, and machines. We have factories on every corner that work around the clock. We work nonstop to increase our endless stock."

Princess Terra replied, "We've heard of King Abaddon. If your factories run non-stop, when do the people have time to rest and play?"

Dracos ignored her question and instead began speaking about his unusual machine. "My machine can find treasures both new and old. Did you know beneath the ground there is hidden black gold?"

Hearing this, Princess Terra replied, "Yes, we know of the black gold. It has been part of the land from ages past."

Officer Dracos interrupted, saying, "Well, King Abaddon is going to buy your land because he wants more black gold. If you leave, he will offer you this big bag of gold."

Princess Terra politely refused, saying, "No, thank you. We don't need your bag of gold. We do not want to sell our land."

Officer Dracos frowned. He grumbled, "Okay then, the king will offer you two bags of gold."

Princess Terra once again graciously refused. "No, thank you. We want to take care of our land and keep living here for years to come."

Dracos raised his voice. "Fine! I will give you three bags of gold from King Abaddon. This is my final offer!" he said with a huff.

The princess smiled and said, "Officer Dracos, please tell King Abaddon that we do not want his gold." She continued her reply to Dracos with a song:

As we were told from days of old
Our land is never to be sold
Your gold may look shiny and bright
But won't keep us warm for many a night
It won't fill our bodies for very long
But the Earth nurtures us in spirit and song
It gives us all we need to live and love
So this is final; we will not budge

Officer Dracos shouted, "How dare you! Since you've refused my offer, King Abaddon will arrive in seven days with his army of venomous snakes." He sneered, "Let's see if you change your mind when you see the king's snakes slither into your land!" He spat on the ground and stomped away.

Princess Terra thought, *Oh dear, what shall I do? What can we do?* So she went to tell her people about King Abaddon's frightening plan.

That evening, the people gathered around the fire. When the children heard about Officer Dracos and King Abaddon's threat, they asked, "Why is this king so greedy? Why does he want to take our land?"

One of the farmers replied,

"The land of Primos is our home

where our children play and freely roam.

We belong here in this place we hold dear,

on this land that has fed us for hundreds of years."

Although they did not want to leave Primos, the people were very scared of King Abaddon's dangerous snakes. The people of Primos had never seen venomous snakes before, so Princess Terra decided to go to her good friend, Princess Saya, for help. Knowing that there was no time to waste, she quickly got ready. Princess Terra rode her swiftest horse, Majestic Wind, to Princess Saya's land.

COMMON CORE DISCUSSION QUESTIONS

Designed for 3rd grade reading level.

1. Describe Princess Mariana. Be sure to provide page numbers as evidence to support your answers. What is her role as a Guardian Princess? (RL.3.1)

2. The setting is important to this story. Look closely at the illustrations and read Mariana's first song again on page 68. Find at least three words or phrases that describe the ocean and why it is important as a setting. (RL.3.1, RL.3.7)

3. Reread the part of the story when Princess Mariana rescues the seal on page 72. The author states on page 73, "We have seen how litter, or *basura,* dumped into *El Mar* has hurt our friends." What does "*basura*" mean? What word could you use to replace it? (RL.3.4, L.3.4) List at least three problems that *basura* is causing. Provide evidence. (RL.3.1)

4. Reread the section of the story when Princess Mariana meets Prince Sujo and the Spumas for the first time on Lixo Island on pages 74-78. Now reread the part when Princess Mariana transforms them on pages 88-91. How do the feelings, actions, and even the names of these characters change as the story progresses? (RL.3.1, RL.3.3, RL. 3.5)

5. What are Fulsi fish? How does Lixo Island impact them? (RL.3.1, RL.3.7)

6. *Princess Mariana and Lixo Island* is the first book in the series to have four princesses working together. Describe how the actions of each princess help change Lixo Island. (RL.3.3)

7. What is the author's central message or lesson in *Princess Mariana and Lixo Island*? Be sure to use key details throughout the story to prove your thinking. (RL.3.2)

Common Core activity pages are available at **www.guardianprincesses.com**

Special Acknowledgements to...

Abigail Micu, Jr.
Agnieszka Wormus-Dziurka
Albert Fetter
Alejandro Cruz
Alfredo Cruz
Alia Murphy
Alicia Marie Castro
Allison Wagner
Alyssa Baden Maroni
Andy & Eileen Wong
Anni Zhang
Arabella Kats
Aria Pulido
Arissa Lau
Arlene Chan
Audrey Harper Zint
Ava & Emi Mracek
Ava Calista Rodriguez Unson
Aysha Rehman
Boone Family Foundation
Brian Kosinski
Briana Campos
Bronwyn Leebaw
Calie
Cassandra Fornazzari
Catriona Chapman
Claire Sullivan
Conna Porcari
Cori Mehring
The Crouse Family
Daniela Coleman
Danielle Collett
Don and Pati Nagai
The Donahue Sisters
Dovie Owens
Dr. Edgardo P. Rodriguez
Eden Aurora Riegle
Elaine K. Herren
Rev. Elizabeth Archer Klein

Elizabeth Horan
Emilia Marie Cooper
Emily, Lauryn & Olivia B.
Esme Belle Blauvelt
Evan Elizabeth Kimsey
Francesca Jones
Gabriella Veenbaas
Gary Hooley
Gina Dent
Greta Young
Havana Maja Kriste
Hoefflinger Family
Ilee
Isabella Kwan
Ivana Marco
Jacqueline Shea Murphy
Jan Chaloner
Jane Ward
Jannali Jaslow
Jennifer Lewis
Jersey Rucker
Jessica
Jihae Cho-Lee
Jocyl Sacramento
Jolie Chea
John and Debi Moore
Jodi Kim
Jules & Ethan Levesque
Julie Pearl
K Sankar & Malathi S.
Narayan
Kacy Fiona
Kaitlyn Huynh
Kaiya Yamane
Karen A. Worden
Karlyn Williams
Karys Rutherford
Katherine Kunberger
Keiko Fukuda

Ken & Sakiko Shigematsu
Kira Murphy
Kloe Garcia
Kori Bartels
L. Ishimitsu
Lan Duong
Lana Frost
Lauren King
Leela Murashige
The Levenberg Family
Lia Payne
Lilliana Collamer
Lily Kira Beitzel
Lucy Ella Patterson
Lynda Foley
Maisie Johnson
Malia Frances
Yi Ling Morioka
Marina Woodward
Marsanne Fetterer
Mary Claire Gatmaitan
Mary Israni
The McHugh Family
Melina Abdullah
Mia McCarty
Mika Ching
Mika Shigematsu
Monica Pearson
Monica-April Skinner
Mylan Gardener
Naoki Shigematsu
Naomi Gagner
Natalie & Nicole Hong
Nitin Govil
Nomi Lee
Norah Nuss
Olivia Guadagnoli
Paola Karina
Princess Gabrielle

Rachel LaManna
Raman Prasad
Ramón Riba
Raul Rodriguez
Restituta Marco
Riley Kay Greeley
Rob Delamater
Robert So
Roselita Jasso
Ruby Senatore
Samantha Nicole Toomey
Samantha Wallace
Samie Cordon
Sandy Liang
Sangeeta Anand
Sarita Echavez See
Scott Madden
Selah Faith Dorn
Skylar Meicho
Henderson Black
Sofia Mann
Sophia Veenbaas
Sormeh Ayari
Spencer Jane White
Susan and Ryan
Susie J. Pak
Tahlia
Tammara Rucker
Tanis Worden
Tara Northrop
Tei Luz Hernández-Day
Tina Flispart
Tung & Mylan Ngo
Una Barraclough
Vanessa Woodley
Wendy A. B. Whipple

Princess Saya lived by a beautiful waterfall at the edge of a rain forest. She was the Guardian of the Lakes and Rivers. She had deep knowledge of reptiles, including those with a venomous bite.

Princess Terra told her friend about King Abaddon's plans. Princess Saya said, "Fear not, my friend. Venomous snakes can be soothed by playing a special song on the flute."

She spent the day teaching Princess Terra how to play a magical song on the flute that had a beautiful soothing melody. Princess Terra practiced and learned it quickly.

She thanked Princess Saya, and they hugged each other good-bye before she rode back to Primos.

As soon as she arrived back in Primos, Princess Terra went to the village. "Everyone, it's time to take out your flutes! I am going to teach you a new song!" she said.

"Princess, how can we enjoy playing music at a time like this? We are so worried that some of us are thinking about fleeing from Primos," a farmer said with a gloomy face. Others were so sad that they had tears in their eyes, for they did not wish to leave their beloved homeland.

Princess Terra said, "Don't worry, my friends. I have learned a special song from Princess Saya that will keep us safe from King Abaddon's snakes." The farmers got their flutes and sat with Princess Terra to learn the new song.

With the day approaching of King Abaddon's frightening arrival, everyone practiced very diligently.

Sure enough, on the seventh day, Officer Dracos and King Abaddon arrived with soldiers carrying large jars of dangerous snakes. The king declared, "Since you did not sell me your land, I am going to release these snakes in Primos and force you to leave. Then, the land will be all mine!"

With trembling hands, the soldiers opened their jars, and hundreds of snakes slithered out. The largest snakes were king cobras, and they were hissing loudly. A few of the soldiers were so scared that they ran away screaming, "AAAHH! HELP!"

The king stood on a platform and declared,

"These venomous snakes will attack anyone in sight.
They are under my magic spell to slither and bite.
I am the mighty King Abaddon, and don't you forget.
I take everything I want, and whatever I want I get."

To the king's surprise, Princess Terra and the people did not run in fear, but instead they sat bravely as the snakes slithered near. Princess Terra smiled as she took out her flute, and her people followed suit. As they began to play in perfect harmony, the sound grew and grew and grew!

The soothing melody was the most beautiful song they'd ever played. As the sound of music echoed across the hills, the snakes stopped slithering and soon fell asleep. The magical music was able to break the king's evil spell.

The king cried, "What has happened to my dangerous snakes?! They were under my spell. What have you done?!"

He shouted at the remaining soldiers, "Take away their flutes! What are you waiting for?!" The soldiers were hesitant because they too enjoyed the peaceful melody.

As the farmers continued to play the song, Princess Terra said, "King Abaddon, you are not welcome here. It is wrong to use these snakes to carry out your evil deeds. Until you learn to respect all living beings and our way of life, do not return to Primos."

The king said, "You may have outsmarted me, Princess, but this is not the end."
He shouted to Dracos and the soldiers, "Pick up my useless sleeping snakes!"

That very afternoon, King Abaddon returned to Voracity.

The people cheered, "Hooray, the wicked King Abaddon is gone! Hail to Princess Terra and the power of the song!"

Princess Terra humbly said, "Thank you, but I did not do this alone. My good friend, Princess Saya, shared her knowledge and taught me the special song, and you all practiced diligently and performed it beautifully. Let's invite her to our autumn music festival!"

On the day of the festival, as the farmers were preparing for the feast, two of King Abaddon's soldiers nervously crawled out of the nearby bushes. They saw the princess and asked, "Can we stay with you in the land of Primos? We don't want to go back to Voracity. We promise to never harm the people or the land again."

Princess Terra said, "You are welcome to join our community. You must be hungry. Come and eat!"

The soldiers jumped with joy, bowed to the princess, and ran toward the food. During the festival, all the people enjoyed the delicious food that they had prepared for each other. They sang and danced to their hearts' content.

As the festival came to a close, Princess Terra thanked everyone for working together to foil King Abaddon's wicked plan.

She said, "Princess Saya helped us stop the greedy king. Like her, we should also do our best to help and protect others in need." As the sun set over Primos, everyone made a circle, held hands, and sang together in unison:

We pledge to do what is just and fair
To do our best to protect and care
For all living beings great and small have worth
We shall come together to take care of our Earth
We have seen what friendship and unity can bring
We were able to stop the selfish, greedy king
We shall protect the seas, skies, and lands of all nations
To be cherished and shared by the next generations

This became their promise and the new pledge of the Guardian Princesses.

The End

The princess and the other farmers were excited for the Harvest Jubilee. This is the day when all the people of the kingdom come together to give thanks for the trees and plants and gather food from the garden. They all woke up early in the morning to start preparing for the celebration.

As they decorated the garden with colorful lanterns and streamers, a mysterious man driving a big red carriage passed through the village square. He did not stop or speak to anyone but instead rode on toward the king's castle.

Later that afternoon, while everyone was away from the garden, a thousand hungry caterpillars came and ate all of the fruits and vegetables. They ate and ate and ate! They devoured all of the fresh crops from the village garden all the way to the king's castle.

King Usambara was the ruler of Amani, and he also had a big garden filled with delicious fruits and vegetables. The king's gardener rushed into the court and screamed, "Your Majesty! All of the fruits and vegetables in the garden are gone!"

King Usambara exclaimed, "WHAT?! That was our entire supply of food! How can this be?!"

The gardener responded, "I don't know, sir. I don't know how this could have happened. What shall I do?"

Just then they heard a menacing voice from the doorway and saw the mysterious carriage driver. He said, "I know what you can do."

"Who are you? How did you get in here?" the king forcefully asked.

"Never fear, Your Majesty. I'm here to help you.
You're upset about your food, but I know what to do.
Your garden has a bad case of the Gulavores.
They eat and eat and still want more!
They're greedy caterpillars who eat everything in sight.
They will eat everything until the very last bite."

"How do you know this? Who are you? What is your name?" asked the king.

The mysterious man said in a sly tone,

"My name is Danga and I come from the cold land of Gullon,

where I make fruits and vegetables with my mighty wand.

I'm a sorcerer who touches the soil of many lands.

I create plants and food with my own two hands.

I can bring plenty for each child, woman, and man.

Lend me your ear, and I will tell you my plan."

Meanwhile, Princess Vinnea and the farmers returned to the garden to continue preparing for the Harvest Jubilee. As they entered the village garden, they saw that the crops were gone! All that remained were scraps of fruits and vegetables. Everyone was upset, and some children even began crying.

Princess Vinnea asked, "What happened to our garden? This was our only food supply."

Danga suddenly appeared from the crowd and said, "Don't worry, Princess. My name is Danga, and I come from the land of Gullon. I have enough food for all the people of the village. My food is very special and will make you feel satisfied."

Princess Vinnea asked, "What kind of food is this? Our people eat food only from the Earth."

Danga went to his carriage and pulled out an apple. The apple was the size of three regular apples.

"This is similar to the apple that is made from the ground,
but this one has been made bigger, shinier, and perfectly round.
I have enough for the whole village. Look at the huge potatoes,
giant strawberries, plump peaches, and enormous tomatoes.
I have pears the size of pigeons and gigantic grapes galore.
I have such an abundance! You'll be amazed by my store.
Give my food a try, it will make an amazing meal.
And don't worry, I'll give you an unbelievable deal.
My supply of food is endless! Come take what you need.
Take all that you want from my carriage and eat! Eat! EAT!"

At first, the people of the kingdom were very sad that all of their food was gone. However, after seeing the huge fruits and vegetables, they praised Danga and took food from his carriage. Princess Vinnea was not impressed. She was suspicious. Something did not seem right to her.

One of the farmers suggested, "Let's have the Harvest Jubilee in honor of Danga!" Everyone cheered in agreement except Princess Vinnea.

She thought to herself, *It is not natural for fruits and vegetables to be so big.* Rather than eat Danga's food, she decided to eat the leaves of the Brumie trees.

47

Sure enough, after the farmers ate Danga's food, they began to get sick, and terrible sores grew on their skin.

Worried about her people, Princess Vinnea
wrote a letter to her friend Princess Terra
and asked her to come right away.

When Princess Terra arrived, she and Princess Vinnea returned to the garden. They were sad to see it so empty. They planted seeds into the soil, and together they said,

"What happened to our beautiful garden that we cherish?
Please grow back the fruits and vegetables, so our people won't perish.
We love how your food makes us healthy and strong.
Please return to normal. Help us prove Danga wrong."

Suddenly, a strange noise came from one of the bushes.

"Munch! Munch! Munch!"

Princess Terra looked closer and exclaimed, "Princess Vinnea, look at this caterpillar! This is a Gulavore. They eat everything in sight. They come from the land of Gullon."

Princess Vinnea said, "Gullon? That is where Danga comes from. I bet that he brought them here to destroy our gardens."

"But why?" Princess Terra asked.

Princess Vinnea replied, "I think that he wants us to buy his big fruits and vegetables. But something must be wrong with them because they make the people sick."

The two princesses found Danga's carriage. Inside, Princess Vinnea picked up a big red book titled *Magic Spells for Plants and Bugs*. As the princesses looked through the book, they found the magic spell that Danga used for making his unusual fruits and vegetables. The spell mixed magic with toxic chemicals.

Princess Vinnea said, "I know that there are good and helpful chemicals, but Danga's are harmful."

Princess Terra said, "His food is not made with love. What kind of person would make food that makes people sick?"

Princess Vinnea said, "We must stop the people from eating Danga's food!"

Princess Terra added, "Let's take his spell book, so he can't use it to do any more harm."

In the spell book they also found a page about the Gulavores. "Look, here is how to get rid of the Gulavores in the garden. All we have to do is sing this song."

Gula! Gula! Gula!
Bellies full of leaves
Gula! Gula! Gula!
Time to fly beyond the trees!

Even though the people were sick, they still wanted to celebrate the Harvest Jubilee. King Usambara came to the village square to honor Danga.

At the same moment, Princess Vinnea and Princess Terra arrived.
Princess Vinnea announced, "Do not eat the food that Danga gave you. His food is the reason you have all become so sick! He brought Gulavores from his homeland to attack our garden, so that he can sell us his dangerous food!"

"No, I'm here to help you," Danga said. "These fruits and vegetables make you feel full. They are good for you!"

Princess Vinnea said, "No, these fruits and vegetables are not good for the people! They're dangerous! Admit it, Danga. You ruined our garden in order to sell us this unhealthy food!"

Danga said, "I have nothing to admit."

"Princess Vinnea," King Usambara said as he walked toward her, "even if what you say is true, if we planted new seeds in the garden today, we will have to wait many months for the crops to grow."

"Don't worry. Just follow us to the village garden," Princess Vinnea said.

When they arrived, the Gulavores were everywhere! They were all over the garden. The princesses sang the magic spell together:

Gula! Gula! Gula!
Bellies full of leaves
Gula! Gula! Gula!
Time to fly beyond the trees!

All of a sudden, the Gulavores turned into beautiful, colorful butterflies. The garden was filled with a rainbow of butterflies.

The princesses continued singing:

Gula! Gula! Gula!
Carrying sweetness like bees
Gula! Gula! Gula!
Time to fly beyond the trees!

The butterflies began flying around the garden. Glitter fell from their shimmery wings onto the soil as they fluttered through the air. Plants began sprouting from the ground. The garden quickly grew beautiful flowers, fruits, and vegetables.

Danga cried, "How can this be?"

Princess Vinnea replied, "We used your magic book to break your spell, Danga!"

"That's right!" Princess Terra added. "The Earth has helped the people once again. The wing dust of the butterflies fertilized the garden, and its magic made all the plants grow quickly!"

Danga screamed, "No! You have ruined my plans!" He started to run away toward the Brumie woods.

"Not so fast!" Princess Vinnea said. She opened up the spell book and sang:

Seeds and soil, you reap what you sow
Greed and spoil, fake food is what you grow
Leaves fallen from trees, dirt to mud
Turn the wicked Danga into a bug!

Danga was instantly transformed into a dung beetle. Princess Vinnea quickly scooped him up and dropped him into a jar. "Now, my little friend, you can no longer harm anyone." All the people cheered! The village garden began flourishing again and was more beautiful than ever.

Princess Vinnea announced, "Everyone, please enjoy the new fruits and vegetables that our garden has given us today." The villagers ran to the garden with great excitement. Everyone ate the fresh crops, and by eating the fresh fruit and vegetables, those who were sick from eating Danga's food were healed.

King Usambara thanked Princess Vinnea and Princess Terra for saving the village garden. He asked, "Would you restore my garden too? I would be forever grateful."

Princess Vinnea said, "We would love to, and now that the garden is restored, let's finally have our Harvest Jubilee!"

That day was the busiest and happiest Harvest Jubilee in the history of Amani. Princess Vinnea turned Danga's food into stones that the people used to decorate the garden. Everyone had a merry time. They ate and played music to celebrate the garden and the princesses' victory. They danced and sang this song to thank the Earth for providing an abundance of plentiful, healthy food, as the sun set over the beautiful garden:

We pledge to do what is just and fair
To do our best to protect and care
For all living beings great and small have worth
We shall come together to take care of our Earth
Growing strong like a tree from healthy food
We will nurture the garden because it nourishes us too
We shall protect the seas, skies, and lands of all nations
To be cherished and shared by the next generations

The End

ETYMOLOGY CHART

Etymology: the origin of a word

Name	Language	Meaning
Amani	Swahili	peace
Danga	Swahili	shortened from *kudanganya*, which means "deceit"
Gulavore	Latin	*gula* means "gluttony" "-vore" is the suffix for "eat, consume, devour" thus *gula*+vore = Gulavores
Usambara	Shambala	named after the Usambara Mountains in northeast Tanzania; means land of the Sambaa
Vinnea	Latin	*vinea* means "vine" added extra 'n' for pronunciation

GLOSSARY

Abundance: a large amount of something

Bountiful: large in quantity; plentiful

Chemical: a natural or artificial substance that has a particular composition. All matter is made of chemicals

Cherish: to feel love for; to hold dear

Dung beetle: a type of beetle that eats animal manure (poop). Some kinds of dung beetles bury manure, helping fertilize the soil

Fertilized: to add fertilizer (a natural or manufactured substance added to soil to help plants grow)

Harvest: the season when crops are gathered; the gathering of crops

Lantern: a light that can be carried around

Menacing: threatening or suggesting possible danger

Plump: having a full, round shape

Sorcerer: a wizard or warlock who practices magic

COMMON CORE DISCUSSION QUESTIONS

Designed for 3rd grade reading level.

1. Describe Princess Vinnea's character traits. Provide evidence from the text to support your answer. (RL.3.3)

2. How do the Gulavores contribute to the story? (RL.3.1, RL.3.3) Look at the etymology chart. Why do you think the author chose this Latin name for them?

3. The author uses the words sly and mysterious to describe Danga. Determine the meaning of these words using clues from the story and illustrations. What words could you replace them with? (RL.3.4, RL.3.7, L.3.4)

4. Explain how the illustrations of Danga emphasize his character traits. Provide evidence to show how words and phrases in the story are expressed through the illustrations. (RL.3.7)

5. Reread the parts of the story that discuss the Harvest Jubilee. What do you think a jubilee is? What clues from the story help you to understand this word? What word could you replace jubilee with? (RL.3.4, L.3.4)

6. How does the mood of the people in Amani change throughout the story? Provide evidence from several parts of the story to support your answer. (RL.3.3, RL.3.5)

7. What is the author's central message or lesson in *Princess Vinnea and the Gulavores*? Be sure to use key details in the story to prove your thinking. (RL.3.2)

Common Core activity pages are available at **www.guardianprincesses.com**

PRINCESS Mariana AND LIXO ISLAND

WRITTEN BY
ASHANTI MCMILLON
& THE GUARDIAN PRINCESS ALLIANCE

ILLUSTRATED BY A. DAS

 NCE UPON A TIME there was a smart and caring princess named Mariana. She lived in the kingdom of Armonía. It was a beautiful island with tall palm trees, warm sands, and an abundance of fruit trees. Princess Mariana was the Guardian of the Seas. She could talk to all of the sea creatures, from the tiniest seahorses to the biggest blue whales. Every day, she would run to the beach and swim with her sea friends to explore the ocean. Princess Mariana would sing:

El Mar is our magnificent home
With endless waves where we can roam
Clear blue seas shimmering in the sun
A place where sea creatures can all have fun
A home with joy and energy
A place where we can all be free
We love the agua, we love the sea
I'll take care of you, as you take care of me

El Mar: Spanish for "the sea"
Agua: Spanish for "water"

The land and sea creatures in the kingdom were called Armonians, and they lived together in perfect harmony. The seas surrounding Armonía were filled with Fulsi fish. Whenever the Fulsi fish were happy, their scales glittered. The sea was so clean and pure that it shimmered from the Fulsis' colorful, shining scales. They could breathe air, walk on land, and make the waves glow with their glittering scales.

A Fulsi fish named Iris was Princess Mariana's best friend. They would go on adventures together, along with their good friend Feliz, the fastest dolphin in the kingdom. Feliz always gave them rides on his back to any part of the ocean that they wished to explore.

One day, Princess Mariana, Iris, and Feliz were in the ocean playing with the sea turtles. As the sea turtles were telling stories about their ancestors, a voice cried from the distance. "HELP! I'm trapped! Someone help me! I can't move!"

Princess Mariana and her friends quickly swam toward the voice and found a seal caught inside a black rubber tire. "This is very dangerous! We must rescue him from that trap!" exclaimed the sea turtle. They all worked together to free the seal.

"Thank you so much," said the exhausted seal. "I was so scared. I was just swimming through the waves, and then suddenly I was caught in this awful trap."

One of the sea turtles said, "That trap is called a tire. It does not belong in the ocean. Unfortunately, people litter the oceans every day with tires, garbage, and many other kinds of trash. We have seen how litter, or *basura*, dumped into *El Mar* hurts our friends."

"Yes, litter often traps and harms our sea friends," said the other sea turtle. "We also sometimes think it's food and accidentally eat it, which makes us very sick. Anything that does not belong in the sea is pollution. There are also many islands polluted with litter."

"Something must be done!" exclaimed Princess Mariana. "We cannot have islands covered with litter polluting our beautiful oceans and harming sea creatures! Mr. Seal, where were you swimming?" she asked.

The seal said, "I swam by an island covered with litter. It is called Lixo Island. I can take you to it."

"Yes please! Let's go right away. *¡Vámonos!*" Princess Mariana said.

Basura: Spanish for "garbage"
Vámonos: Spanish for "let's go"

73

They soon arrived at an island covered with garbage and slime. When they saw the island, tears came to their eyes. Princess Mariana and her friends had never seen such waste. It was a horrible place.

Then they heard the sound of footsteps sloshing in the slime. A crowd of dark figures arose from the trash heaps and walked towards them. One of the tall dark figures said, "Who goes there? Who dares to cross the sands of Lixo Island?"

"My name is Princess Mariana, Guardian of the Seas," she said confidently. "I am here with my sea friends to find out why the ocean is being polluted with litter. We came here to stop this from happening!"

The tall dark figure began laughing. "You think you can stop this? Well, you are wrong! My name is Prince Sujo, ruler of the Spumas of Lixo Island. I was appointed by King Abaddon, ruler of Voracity, to be in charge of collecting his kingdom's garbage and waste."

Princess Mariana replied, "There's so much garbage here that it is overflowing into the ocean. Surely not all of these things are waste. Do you know that bottles, cans, and many other things can be recycled and turned into new things? We can help you clean it up."

Prince Sujo walked out of the shadows and said, "This island has too much trash for anyone, even a powerful princess, to remove!" He continued,

"Just look at the old rubber tires by the wilting trees,
with no fruit, few branches, and certainly no leaves.
Broken glass and plastic bags are scattered everywhere,
tattered shoes that no one would ever care to wear.
We have crushed soda cans and six-pack rings,
plastic bottles, Styrofoam, and other disgusting things.
Junk and chunks of compacted trash,
this is where Voracity's waste is stashed."

Princess Mariana responded, "It is wrong for King Abaddon to dump waste on your home. Your people are suffering! Why don't you stand up to him? We can help you." Prince Sujo said, "There is nothing that can be done!" He summoned the other dark figures. "Spumas, tell this princess who you are!"

The slimy and dirty Spumas began to sing:

Spumas! Spumas! That is who we are
We live on a dirty island made from garbage and tar
Spumas! Spumas! We swim in thick black oil
That King Abaddon dumped here, leaving trash to rot and spoil

Prince Sujo turned to the princess and said, "Now, I suggest you leave. You have no business here."

"This island is a danger to you, the Spumas, and all of our sea friends. We shall leave for now but will soon return to Lixo Island. We must keep the waters clean!" Princess Mariana said. She turned away and jumped on Feliz's back, and they returned to Armonía.

As they approached Armonía Island, Princess Mariana noticed that the Fulsi fish were no longer glowing. The *basura* in the water was making them all sick. Iris said, "Princess, we are not happy. We must find a way to remove this litter soon or else the glowing power of the Fulsi fish will be lost for good."

Princess Mariana paced back and forth as she pondered what to do. *I need help from my friends*, she thought, so she sent three messenger birds asking her friends to come quickly.

The next morning, Princess Mariana heard the sound of a strong gust of wind. She ran outside and saw Princess Terra, Princess Vinnea, and Princess Ten Ten descending on a cloud.

Princess Mariana exclaimed, "Thank you for coming, friends! I really need your help!" She told them about how King Abaddon had turned Lixo Island into a wasteland. She explained how its trash was spreading across the sea to Armonía and beyond.

Princess Terra said, "I know about King Abaddon's dirty deeds. He must be stopped."

Princess Vinnea nodded. "Yes. We have to get rid of this pollution. But how?"

"We can work together to remove the garbage from Lixo Island," Princess Mariana said. Then she began explaining her plan…

The next day, Princess Mariana and her friends arrived at Lixo Island. A big ship with "VORACITY WASTE" printed on its side was docked by the shore. The Spumas were unloading the trash from the ship and throwing it onto the island.

Princess Mariana called out, "Prince Sujo, where are you? We are back!"

Prince Sujo walked off the ship and sneered, "Oh, look at what we have here. What do you want now?"

"My friends and I have come to get rid of the *basura* on this island," she responded.

Prince Sujo laughed. "That's impossible. You are foolish for trying."

The Spumas marched toward the princesses and chanted:

We are the Spumas
Covered in dirt and grime
Listen to Prince Sujo, and hear our rhyme
It is impossible for you to clean this place
The mess is everywhere, even on our face
You can't clean this mess or stop it from smelling
Just give up now and go back to your dwelling

The princesses stood their ground and began to carry out their plan.

Princess Mariana began to blow through her favorite conch shell. The sound echoed across the sea, summoning her sea friend, Humberto, the big blue whale.

Princess Ten Ten, Guardian of the Skies, flew towards the clouds and began to create a big gust of wind, singing:

Mighty winds come and go
Lift the dirty trash below

As the trash began whirling into the sky, Princess Terra, Guardian of the Land, knelt down, touched the black sand, and sang:

Dear precious Earth, heal this sand
Bring forth the clean and natural land

The black oil covering the sands rose and floated into Princess Ten Ten's wind ball. The sand was now sparkling clean. Meanwhile, Princess Mariana, Guardian of the Seas, stood in the slimy dark waters. She closed her eyes and sang:

Tides that ebb and flow, push and pull
Let these waters become clean, and the color azul

The sludge and slime lifted from the ocean and swirled into the wind ball. The ocean was now clean and bright blue. Then, from deep beneath the waves, Humberto rose to the surface. "Bring in the water!" Princess Mariana told the whale. From his blowhole, he began to shoot sea water high into the air. Princess Ten Ten motioned a big gust of wind to blow the water onto the trees to clean them.

Then, Princess Vinnea, Guardian of Plant Life, walked over and touched one of the trees. She closed her eyes and sang:

Tree to tree, fruits come alive
Vine to vine, plant life be revived

Azul: Spanish for "blue"

The rotten food that was still lying on the sands sank beneath the moist ground. Suddenly, the plants and trees started to grow bright green leaves. Coconuts, mangoes, and pineapples appeared. The island now looked as bountiful as Armonía. "How are you doing this?!" Prince Sujo screamed.

"Prince Sujo, now it's time for you and the Spumas to get cleaned up too!" Princess Mariana said. She took an empty shell and used it to scoop the clean ocean water. She began to sing:

Spumas, Spumas
Dirty on the outside, feeling you're all alone
You're pure on the inside, there's beauty in your corazón!

The grime covering Prince Sujo and the Spumas disappeared, revealing Prince Sujo to be a fine young man and the Spumas to be good people with kind faces. As soon as they were clean, the Spumas began to help pick up the remaining litter on the beaches.

The princesses took the litter from the Spumas and magically turned it into new, useful things. The broken glass became colorful tiles and bowls. The plastic turned into beach toys and beach chairs. The shredded paper turned into pretty lanterns. Meanwhile, the waste contained in the wind ball spun faster and faster until it burst into sparkles that made Lixo Island shine.

Corazón: Spanish for "heart"

King Abaddon's sailors were shocked by how the princess and her companions cleaned the island. Humberto knocked the side of the ship to get the sailors' attention. They were scared by the presence of the big blue whale.

"That's Humberto's way of saying don't pollute our ocean again," Princess Mariana said. "Tell King Abaddon that we are here to protect the sea and all of its marine life." The sailors nodded in fear and awe and quickly sailed back to Voracity as fast as they could.

The Spumas cheered and ran up to the princesses and their sea friends. Prince Sujo said, "We thank you and your friends, Princess Mariana. My real name is Prince Amel. My kingdom was taken over by the greedy King Abaddon when I was a child. He cast a spell on our home and turned it into Lixo Island. We were turned into dirty Spumas."

He continued, "We have been serving him for years not realizing the harm we were causing. You and your friends are true heroes for helping us clean our island and our ocean!"

"You are welcome, Prince Amel," Princess Mariana said, "but our magic alone is not enough. We all must do our part to keep the islands and oceans clean."

Smiling with gratitude, Prince Amel agreed and said, "From this day forth, our home shall be called Renova Island, and my people, Renovians. We will work to keep our home and beaches clean. We will recycle *basura* to take care of the Earth."

"That sounds like the start of a great plan," said Princess Ten Ten.

"In honor of you and your friends, let's have our first celebration as Renova Island today. How does that sound?" asked Prince Amel. Everyone cheered.

That afternoon, they all gathered at the beach. They sang songs and ate the freshly grown fruit. The sea turtles told old stories to the young guppies. Feliz and the other dolphins played in the waves and leaped in the air. The waters of Renova Island were now glowing from the happy Fulsi fish. They all played games and danced.

The Guardian Princesses shared their pledge with Prince Amel and the Renovians.

We pledge to do what is just and fair
To do our best to protect and care
For all living beings great and small have worth
We shall come together to take care of our Earth
We'll care for the ocean and the beauty of the sea
So marine life can flourish, be happy and free
We shall protect the seas, skies, and lands of all nations
To be cherished and shared by the next generations

The End